Sally
and the
Purple
Socks

Sally and the Purple

Socks

Lisze Bechtold

Philomel Books

Patricia Lee Gauch, Editor

PHILOMEL BOOKS   A division of Penguin Young Readers Group.
Published by The Penguin Group.
Penguin Group (USA) Inc., 375 Hudson Street, New York, NY 10014, U.S.A.
Penguin Group (Canada), 90 Eglinton Avenue East, Suite 700, Toronto, Ontario
M4P 2Y3, Canada (a division of Pearson Penguin Canada Inc.).   •   Penguin Books
Ltd. 80 Strand, London WC2R 0RL, England.   •   Penguin Ireland, 25 St. Stephen's
Green, Dublin 2, Ireland (a division of Penguin Books Ltd).   •   Penguin Group (Australia),
250 Camberwell Road, Camberwell, Victoria 3124, Australia (a division of Pearson Australia
Group Pty Ltd).   •   Penguin Books India Pvt Ltd, 11 Community Centre, Panchsheel Park, New
Delhi - 110 017, India.   •   Penguin Group (NZ), 67 Apollo Drive, Rosedale, North Shore 0632,
New Zealand (a division of Pearson New Zealand Ltd).   •   Penguin Books (South Africa) (Pty)
Ltd, 24 Sturdee Avenue, Rosebank, Johannesburg 2196, South Africa.   •   Penguin Books Ltd,
Registered Offices: 80 Strand, London WC2R 0RL, England.

OCT 2 1 2008

Published simultaneously in Canada   •   Manufactured in China by South China Printing Co. Ltd.
Design by Semadar Megged.   •   The artwork was done with a brushed ink line on top of gouache paint.
Library of Congress Cataloging-in-Publication Data
Bechtold, Lisze.   Sally and the purple socks / Lisze Bechtold.   p. cm.   Summary: When her tiny
purple socks start to expand, Sally turns them into a scarf and then curtains, but things soon get out of
hand.   [1. Socks–Fiction. 2. Size–Fiction.] I. Title.   PZ7.B380765Sal 2008   [E]–dc22   2007023649
ISBN 978-0-399-24734-7
10 9 8 7 6 5 4 3 2

For Frances Jean,
    with love.

Sally couldn't wait to try on her new purple socks.

But they were too small.

Then she saw a note: "Once removed from the box, these socks will grow to the size ordered."

"Oops," said Sally. "Did I tell them my size?"

But after some airing, the purple socks fit perfectly.

Sally danced in them.

She cleaned house in them.

She relaxed in her lovely purple socks. Until . . .

"How odd," said Sally. "Now my socks are too big.

But they are so soft."

So . . .

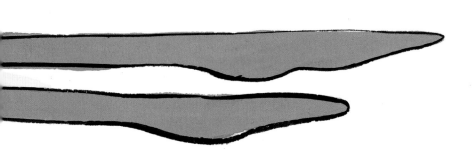

Sally wore her soft purple scarf and cap while she gardened.

But when she came in . . .

"Oh dear!"
quacked Sally.

"Still, they are so cozy."

By lunchtime . . .

Sally grumbled, "This really ruffles my feathers!"

"But . . . they are so warm . . ."

Sally napped under her warm purple blankets. When she woke up . . .

"Now this has got to stop!" quacked Sally.

Sally spent the rest of the day moving furniture.

That night,

she was so tired, she slept on her luxurious purple carpet.

Early the next morning . . .

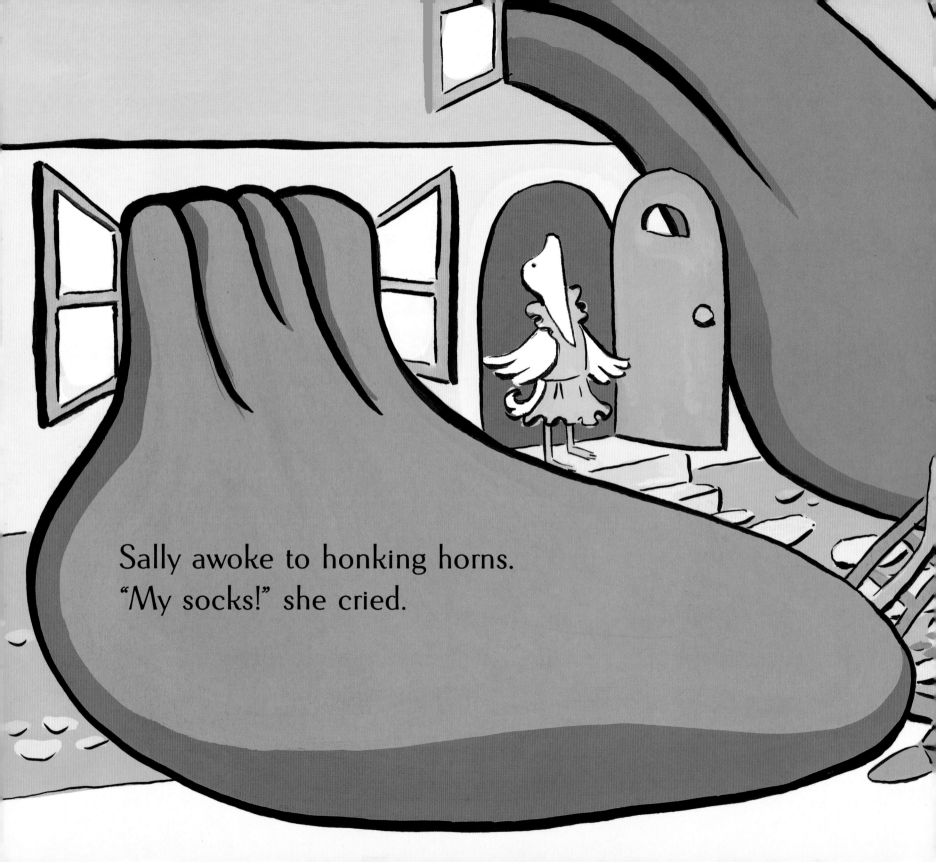

Sally awoke to honking horns.
"My socks!" she cried.

"Your socks are blocking traffic!" hollered the neighbors.

So Sally hauled her socks into
the backyard and invited all her neighbors
to a circus. And everyone came.

When suddenly it began to rain.

It rained,

and rained,

and rained.

Until . . .

Sally's lovely, soft, cozy, warm, luxurious purple socks fit perfectly again!

Just in time for the first snow.